Porter the Hoarder and the Halloween Happening

Porter the Hoarder

For Logan, Quinn & Tommy,
my heart & soul & my very own
little manic monkeys.

—R.S.

I never thought I'd live this long.

—S.C.

And whistles and socks and boas
...and a horse.

ISBN 978-1-7327501-2-8

Hoarding Porter, LLC
PO Box 173
Deadwood, SD 57732

10 9 8 7 6 5 4 3 2 1

Printed in China

One a mummy, two a mummy, three a mummy, WEREWOLF!!

candy-covered eyeball kabobs

crispy crunchy freshly flamed s'mores

pickled patchwork pigeons

gold-wrapped chocolate coins

blood-sucking

biting bats

squeaky clown noses

freshly fried tarantula pop

phlegmy furballs

GLIMMERY SHIMMERY TEA PARTY TIARA!!!!

?

puffy purple popcorn ball

This is Porter.

She's a hoarder.

This is how you know.

Piles of costumes and
Halloween hats

are here for her to show.

What you need to know about Porter is that she is
a sneaky little mongrel who has a perfect plan to
score the best loot from each and every house
in the Monster Neighborhood.

Just last week, Porter and her mom threw away leftovers from last year's Halloween haul. Because of the abundance of mice, mold and mildew that filled up her room, Porter can only bring home one pillowcase full of candy this Halloween.

What Porter's mom doesn't know is that Porter has a plan to get all the finest tricks and treats from the spookiest Halloween houses in town.

If Porter brings home JUST one and
ONLY one pillowcase of goodies,
she gets to have her very own...

PRINCESS TEA PARTY!!!

Can you help her decide which
spooktacular somethings she gets to keep
and which she has to leave behind?

Ready?

Let's

GO!

Porter's first stop in the Monster
Neighborhood is at the haunted mansion
of Wilhelmina the Wicked Witch.

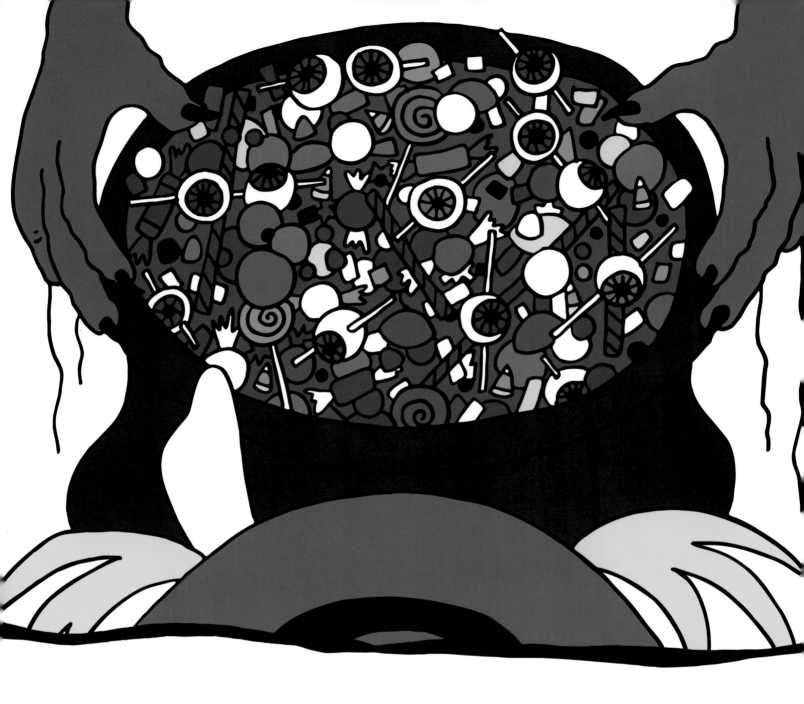

Help Porter find ten candy-covered
eyeball kabobs. Can you find all ten?

Should she keep the 10 candy-covered eyeball kabobs?

Porter's next stop in the Monster Neighborhood is at the cavernous cave of Dave the Deadly Dragon.

Help Porter find nine crispy,
crunchy freshly flamed s'mores.
Can you find all nine?

Should she keep the 9 crispy, crunchy freshly flamed s'mores?

YES!!

Porter's next stop in the Monster Neighborhood is at the creepy castle of Fredrick Thaddeus VonFrankenstein.

Help Porter find eight pickled
patchwork pigeons.
Can you find all eight?

Should she keep the
8 pickled patchwork
pigeons?

No!!!

Porter's next stop in the Monster Neighborhood is at the perilous pirate ship of Creepy Captain Crackenbottom.

Help Porter find seven gold-wrapped
coins. Can you find all seven?

Should she keep the 7 gold-wrapped coins?

YES!

Porter's next stop in the Monster Neighborhood is at the frightening fortress of Jerry the Vicious Vampire.

Help Porter find six blood-sucking
biting bats. Can you find all six?

Should she keep the 6 blood-sucking biting bats?

NO.

Porter's next stop in the Monster
Neighborhood is at the hilarious home
of Paco the Carnival Clown.

Help Porter find five squeaky
clown noses. Can you find all five?

Should she keep
the 5 squeaky
clown noses?

YES.

Porter's next stop in the Monster Neighborhood is at the terrible tomb of Murray the Malicious Mummy.

Help Porter find four freshly fried tarantula pops. Can you find all four?

Should she keep the 4 freshly fried tarantula pops?

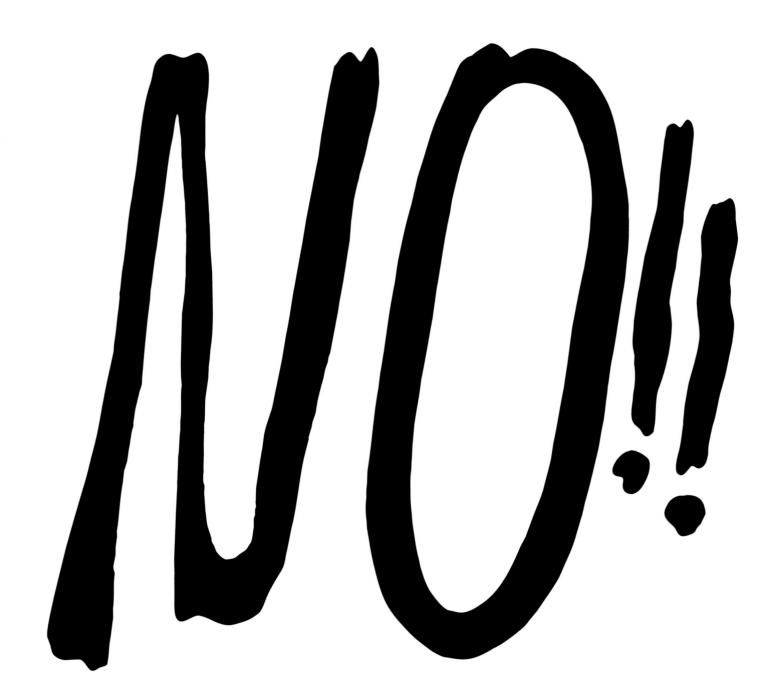

Porter's next stop in the Monster Neighborhood is at the gruesome graveyard of Syrus the Spooky Spector.

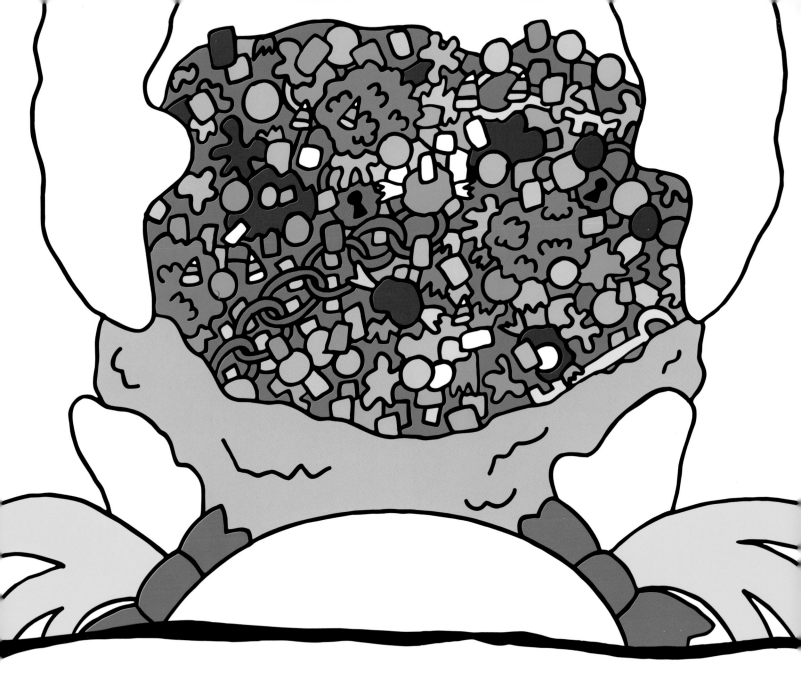

Help Porter find three
puffy purple popcorn balls.
Can you find all three?

Should she keep
the 3 puffy purple
popcorn balls?

YES!

Porter's next stop in the Monster Neighborhood is at the spine-chilling shack of Harry M. McHowler.

Help Porter find two filthy, phlegmy fur balls. Can you find them both?

Should she keep the 2 filthy, phlegmy fur balls?

Thanks to you, Porter has nearly filled her
pillowcase with awesome Halloween treasures.
There's just one stop to go; the palatial palace
of Princess Penelope Pufferbottom.

Can you help Porter find a glimmery, shimmery tea party tiara?

Should she keep it?

The
End.

ABOUT THE AUTHOR

SEAN COVEL is a film and television producer who grew up in a blip of a town in the Black Hills of South Dakota. His credits include *Beneath* for Paramount Pictures, *The 12 Dogs of Christmas* directed by Academy Award Winner, Keith Merrill, and the iconic independent film, *Napoleon Dynamite*.

Together, Sean's movies have played lots of places, won a bunch of awards and whatever, and — most importantly — got nerds prom dates across the globe. He very much wishes that would've been the case when he was in high school.

Sean enjoys shooting movies, writing weirdo children's books with his weirdo friends, and lecturing at universities and film festivals internationally, but he hangs his nunchucks in Deadwood, SD.

ABOUT THE ILLUSTRATOR

REBECCA SWIFT should've had a perfectly reasonable career in a perfectly reasonable field. This is due to having excellent parents. Imagine their concern as their daughter expressed interest in all things "the arts."

In addition to drawing doodles and painting pictures, Rebecca is an established singer-songwriter, having been on American Idol and releasing her first album *North of Normal* later that same year. When not art-ing up the place, Rebecca works as a professional makeup artist. Which is still art. But on faces.

Rebecca is a proud mum to two girls (Quinn and Logan) and a lil dude (Tommy). The three were in no way an inspiration for the *Porter the Hoarder* series. Except that they were. Completely. Logan has a thing for stashing candy that is borderline intervention inspiring. …It's a concern.

Rebecca hangs her many, many (many) hats in Bridgewater, SD.